D0719162

It's not *JUST* a blanket!

Written and illustrated by
ANNALIESE STONEY

BONNEY
PRESS

Published by Bonney Press,
an imprint of Hinkler Books Pty Ltd
45–55 Fairchild Street
Heatherton Victoria 3202 Australia
www.hinkler.com.au

Author and illustrator: Annaliese Stoney

ISBN: 978 1 7436 7828 2

Printed and bound in China

For Steve and my family, for all their cheerleading!

It's not

JUST

a blanket...

Sophia *loved* her blanket **VERY** much.

Everywhere...
and
ANYWHERE
that she and her dog Monty went,
the blanket came too!

Her family didn't understand why.

they said.

But Sophia knew better.

Wriggly
Worm!

MUNCH
MUNCH
It's not JUST a blanket!
It's a...

Slippery stingray!

It's not **JUST** a blanket! It's a...

PIRATE SHIP!
It's not JUST a blanket! Look! It's a...

MAGIC CARPET

And it's not JUST a blanket! It's a...

ROARING LION!

And it's not JUST a blanket! It's a...

SNOOZING

In fact, because it's not
JUST a blanket, it's worth...

EIGHT

NGER!

RRR

PP!

Poor Sophia was very upset.

Monty felt pretty bad, too.

Her brother Clive saw the whole thing.

He told the whole family,

who thought very hard, until eventually they came up with

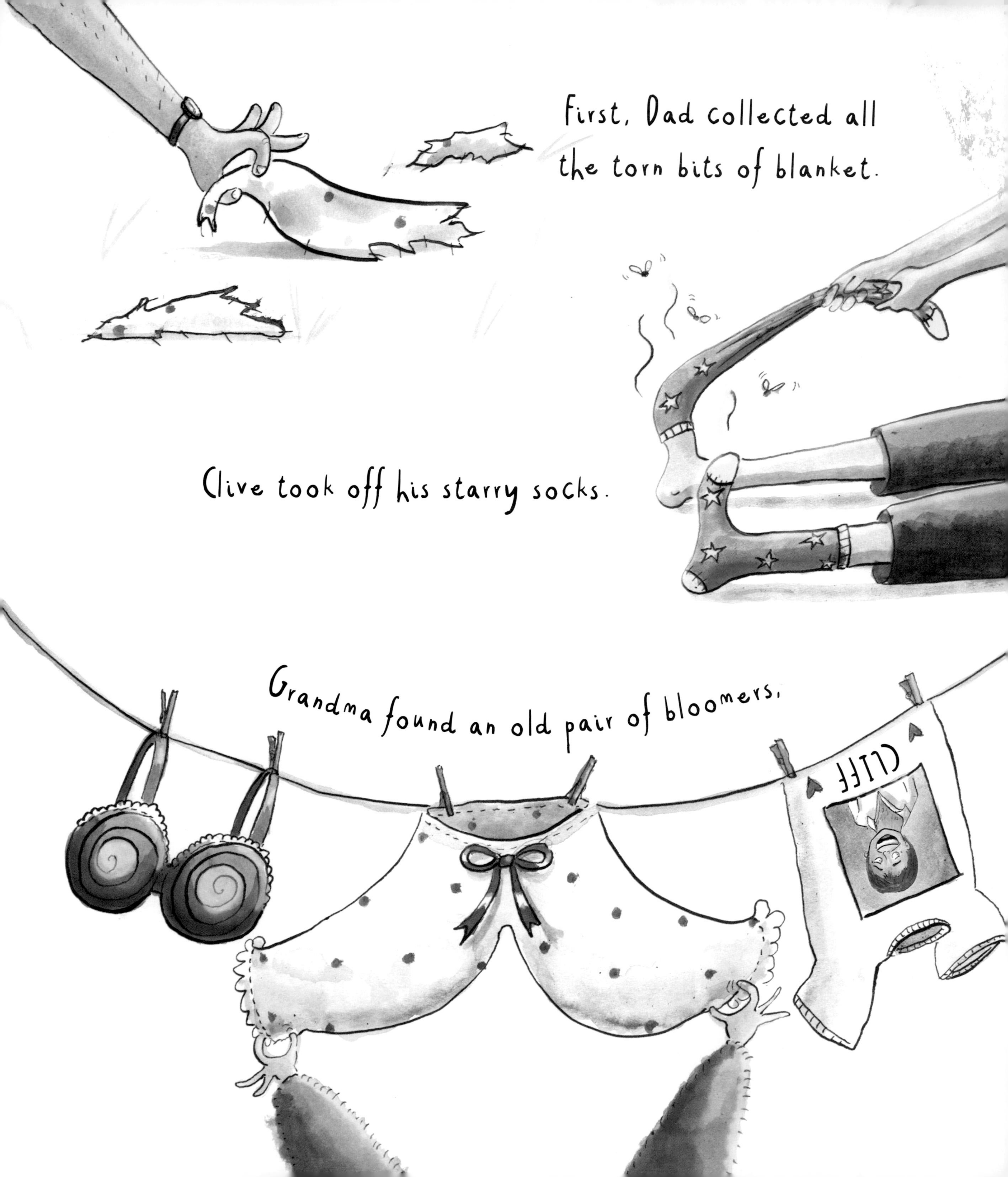

First, Dad collected all the torn bits of blanket.

Clive took off his starry socks.

Grandma found an old pair of bloomers,

and Mom generously donated
Dad's Hawaiian shirt collection.

Then, armed with
a big bundle of
material, they
worked very, very
hard, until...

"TA-DA!" they exclaimed.
"Here you are Sophia and Monty. We know how much you loved that old blanket, so we've made you BOTH new blankets."

"Thank you very much!" Sophia and Monty said.

"The only thing is...

"They're

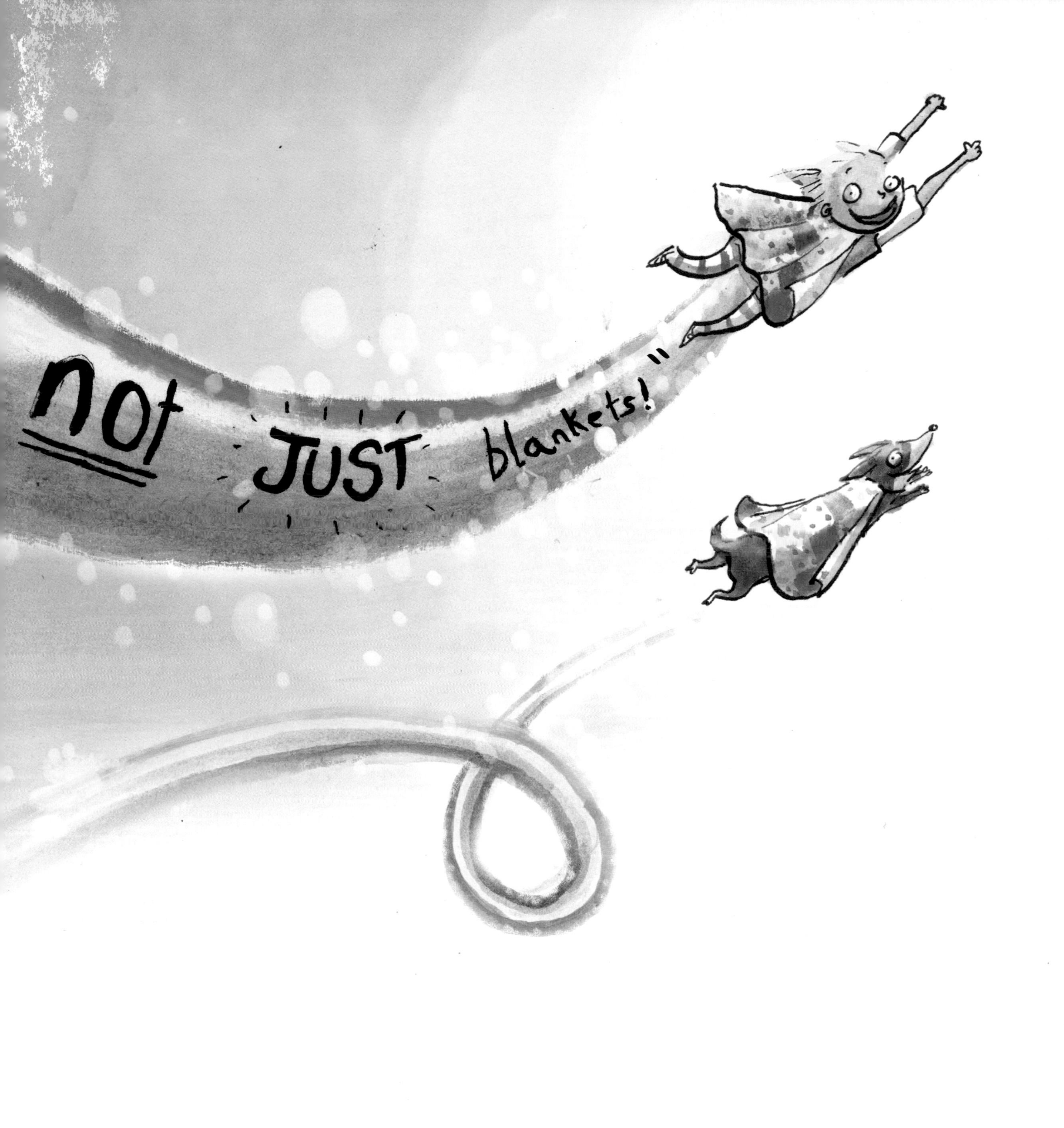
not JUST blankets!"